HE WASN'T THE LOUD ONE

SOME BOYS DON'T RAISE THEIR VOICE, THEY RAISE THEMSELVES.

HUGAR PAVANAKUMAR

To my parents, for their unshakable love.
To my sisters, who helped me understand sensitivity and strength.
To my better half, whose quiet belief shaped this story.
To every friend who came and went—you helped me find my voice.

To all teachers whose teachings derived the better version of ourselves.

In Fond Memory of
Late Major Hubli Sir, whose discipline still echoes in memory.
Late Rahul Sir, whose charisma will always be cherished.

My grandfather, a central inspiration throughout my journey.

And to all the **Aaravs** out there—you are not forgotten.

Contents

Preface

Some stories aren't written to make noise.
They are whispered from memory—told in silences, shared glances, and
the unspoken world of classrooms, chalk dust, and growing pains.

He Wasn't the Loud One is not just a book.
It's a recollection. A quiet tribute to the boys who weren't the toppers, or
the rebels, or the center of attention—but who carried entire worlds inside
them.

It's about friendship and betrayal, favoritism and fairness, unspoken
crushes and silent victories.
It's about Aarav—and everyone who's ever been Aarav at some point in
life.

This book doesn't ask to be read loudly.
It only asks to be felt.

Acknowledgements

To my parents, for their sacrifices and quiet strength.
To my sisters, who shaped my heart and taught me the gentlest truths of growing up.
To my wife, whose belief in my voice gave this story life.
To my teachers, who didn't just teach lessons—but shaped character.
To my friends, past and present, whose memories—both sweet and bitter—left footprints in my journey.

And to every reader who has ever felt unheard:
You matter. You are remembered. You are not alone.

Author's Note

While inspired by the colors and moments of real school life, *He Wasn't the Loud One* is a work of fiction.

xi

All characters, incidents, school settings, and conversations have been fictionalized for narrative impact.
Any resemblance to actual persons—living or otherwise—is purely coincidental.

Some memories inspired these pages.
But the story belongs to itself.

CHAPTER ONE

THE DAY HE WAS LEFT BEHIND

Aarav's world, until then, had been small, safe, and filled with familiar faces. His grandparents' home smelled of turmeric, sandalwood, and safety. His mother's touch was all he had known. But that day, everything changed.

It was his first day of school.

Three kilometers away stood a building he'd never seen from the inside—Saint Joseph's Primary. His mother dressed him carefully that morning, pressing down every crease in his shirt and oiling his hair with more care than usual. She pinned his handkerchief to his Shirt Pocket bott and made sure his lunch box was packed tight, with the stuff he liked.

She looked more nervous than him.

Outside the gate, two older village boys stood waiting: Anil and Raju. They were maybe eight or nine, with dust on their shoes and a casual way of slinging their bags. They looked like they belonged. Aarav did not.

His mother crouched beside him and whispered, "These are good boys. They'll take care of you, okay?"

Then, louder, she turned to the boys:
"Anil, Raju... please take care of him. It's his first day. During lunch, help him open his box—it's tight. Sit with him. Eat together."

Anil nodded, almost respectfully. Raju gave a half-smile and shrugged.

Aarav held Anil's hand like it was a rope across a river. His other hand gripped the metal handle of his water bottle. His small feet shuffled nervously as they walked toward the school.

The school was too loud.

Too many colours. Too many faces. Too many unknowns.

The classroom felt like a world of giants. The teacher's voice was harsh and fast. The bench was hard, too tall for his dangling legs. Aarav sat in the first row, eyes wide, mouth silent. He didn't even cry—he just folded into himself.

That first half of the day passed in a haze of confusion and sound. Aarav didn't speak a word. He didn't ask where the toilet was. He didn't answer when the teacher called roll. He just kept looking sideways—at Anil.

During lunch, as promised, Anil returned.

He came into the class, sat beside him, and gently pulled the metal clips of the tight lunchbox. Aarav's face lit up—not because of the food, but because someone had remembered. Anil didn't say much. He just ate next to Aarav, sharing water and glancing at the teacher's table when she looked away.

That moment—however small—meant everything.

But the day wasn't done.

When school ended, the boys regrouped to walk home. The shortcut route—the one that led through the riverbed—was faster. Anil and Raju whispered with the other older boys. Aarav followed, not because he wanted to, but because he had no one else.

The rocks were slippery. His bag was heavy. His water bottle swung like a pendulum, slapping his chest. His pants slipped with each step, and he had to keep pulling them up with one hand.

Then, without warning—

"Snake! Snake!" someone screamed.

Panic exploded.

Boys screamed. Feet splashed. Bags dropped. Everyone ran.

Everyone... except Aarav.

He tried. His tiny legs moved, but the wet stone betrayed him.

He slipped.

His back slammed into the riverbed. Water soaked him. His water bottle thudded against his ribs. His pants nearly fell off. His hands reached out—to nothing.

"Wait for me!" he cried.

But no one stopped.

He saw their backs disappearing.

And they kept going.

When Aarav finally scrambled up the muddy bank, scratched and soaked, he didn't cry anymore. His throat had already given up. When he started walking collecting all his things. He heard laughter in the woods, no help but amusement. They had seen him fall. They had heard him cry.

But the pain wasn't in his knees. It was in the realization that the boy who had helped open his lunchbox—Anil—was now walking away, laughing with the others.

What had changed?

Was it Raju's influence? The older boy's boldness always seemed to dominate the softer voice of Anil.

As they neared the village entrance, Aarav saw them waiting—not out of concern, but because they knew they'd be asked.

"Aarav," Anil said, trying to sound casual. "We waited for you."

"We didn't mean to leave you," Raju added with a forced smile. "The others ran first. We just followed."

They were lying.

Aarav knew it.

But he said nothing.

When they reached home, his mother rushed out, shocked to see him soaked, dirty, and shivering.

"What happened to you?" she cried, holding his face in her palms.

Before Aarav could speak, Anil stepped in.

"He slipped near the riverbed, Aunty. But we helped him up."

Raju nodded.

Aarav stood still, water dripping from his cuffs, lips trembling. His mother believed them. His grandfather grunted something about small kids walking too far. The moment passed.

But something inside Aarav did not.

That night, lying on his side, he thought of Anil. The boy who had opened his box. The boy who didn't stop.

He didn't hate him. But he couldn't trust him again—not fully.

He had a soft corner, yes. But he never forgot the silence.

And as for Raju, Aarav built a wall that never fell.

That was the day Aarav learned what betrayal felt like—not from enemies, but from those entrusted by your mother.

"The quietest moments carve the deepest truths."

CHAPTER TWO

FAREWELL, FRIENDS

Nothing changed.

That was the worst part.

Aarav had hoped the riverbed incident would pass like a brief summer storm—loud, wet, but quickly forgotten. But it didn't. Because Anil and Raju didn't let it.

By the very next morning, Aarav had become the classroom's newest legend.

He hadn't even opened his mouth when the giggles began.

"Did you hear what Anil anna said? Aarav cried for help like a movie heroine!"

"Raju told it like a full action scene! He slipped and flew into the river like Superman gone wrong!"

"Pants almost fell, da!"

Laughter followed. Even though none of them had been there.

It wasn't his classmates who had seen it—it was Anil, a senior, and Raju, older by a few years. But somehow, their version of the story had trickled down like gospel.

And the boys in Aarav's class, especially those who lived near Anil or looked up to Raju, picked up the story like it was a juicy joke served hot.

That's what hurt more.

The story was carried down from the ones he looked up to.

And now, even the friends Aarav once trusted—boys from his own class—began to shift away, quietly choosing laughter over loyalty.

He noticed it in the small things. How their laughter paused when he walked past. How they whispered and turned away. How even the space on the bench beside him began to disappear.

But not all boys turned away.

In the last row of the classroom sat boys who didn't chase popularity—Imran, Joel, and Raghu. They weren't loud. They weren't leaders. But they weren't cruel either.

Aarav began to find his space among them—not suddenly, but gently, like water finding its way between stones.

One afternoon, Aarav had forgotten his lunch. He sat quietly, pretending to open an empty box just to avoid the embarrassment.

Imran, sitting nearby, tapped him on the shoulder.
"Want an omelette?"

He didn't wait for Aarav to answer. He just tore his omelette in half and slid it into Aarav's box like it belonged there. There were no words. But that's how Imran was—his kindness didn't need noise.

Joel was different—full of talk, always smiling. One day, he leaned over during art class and said,

"Come home after school. Shaktimaan's on. No rain lines today—Dad fixed the antenna."

That evening, Aarav sat cross-legged in Joel's small home, eating puffed rice and watching the superhero spin into flames. They laughed, mimicked Gangadhar, and argued over which villain they'd defeat first.

On weekends, they played cricket—not with a full team, but with a plastic bat and a tired rubber ball. Sometimes Joel's little sister was the umpire. Sometimes the wall decided the match.

And during school breaks, they became inseparable.

While other groups ran wild on the open ground, Aarav and his quiet circle would gather under the shade of the Nilgiri trees, where dry leaves scattered like old pages. That was their corner. Their sanctuary.

There, they played lagori—stacking flat stones and breaking them apart with a rubber ball, yelling, ducking, and collapsing into laughter.

Soon, the circle widened. Two girls—Nimmi and Sharanya, quiet but bold in their own way—started joining the lagori sessions. So did Yusuf, who stammered a bit but never missed a catch, and Bala, the class's slowest runner but sharpest strategist.

Together, they made a strange, beautiful bunch. Not popular. Not powerful. But bound by something better—acceptance without judgment.

They teased each other without meanness. Shared biscuits. Raced to the tap for water. Sat on the dusty cement edge and planned who would bowl next.

It wasn't official.

It wasn't organized.

But it was real.

They didn't talk about pain or loneliness or names like "river boy" or "crybaby." They just... included him. No questions asked.

Imran once said,

"You play better when you're not trying."

It stayed with Aarav.

Because maybe that was the secret to friendship—not trying, just being.

Still, the sting of betrayal lingered.

Anil had helped open his lunchbox.

Anil had been kind.

And yet... Anil had also joined the laughter.

Aarav didn't know what changed.

Was it Raju's influence? Perhaps.

But from that day forward, Aarav never trusted Raju again.

As for Anil, he would always remain in a strange corner of Aarav's heart. Not as a friend. Not as an enemy. Just... someone he couldn't forget.

Then, just as quietly as they had entered his life, Imran and Joel were gone.

Joel's father got a transfer to another city. Imran's family shifted to another town near their relatives. There was no farewell party. No handshakes. Just sudden absence.

Aarav didn't cry.

But that week, he didn't touch his tiffin.

He didn't play lagori.

He just sat under the Nilgiri trees, listening to the rustling above—like someone whispering secrets only he could hear.

So, Aarav adapted. He learned to live in the middle.

He wasn't anyone's favorite.

He wasn't anyone's rival.

He wasn't loud, but he was listening.

And in that quiet space between ridicule and recognition, Aarav discovered something else entirely:

Belonging without explanation.

"Some goodbyes stay longer than the people who said them."

CHAPTER THREE

THE DEPARTURE OF FRIENDS AND THE RISE OF POLITICS

The world had shifted, and Aarav had learned to shift with it.

It had been two years since Imran and Joel disappeared from his life—one to a family transfer, the other to a distant town. Their absence wasn't noisy; it was quiet, but heavy. Like a song ending mid-verse. And with them, Aarav's laughter had faded too. He still remembered their shared tiffins, the games of lagori under the Nilgiri trees, and those after-school afternoons watching Shaktimaan. Now, those memories lived only in the corners of silence.

He had entered Class 6, not with excitement, but with survival instincts. The school felt colder, the benches harder. He kept to the first bench, not because he was a topper, but because it was quiet. It was safer. No one fought to sit there. No one cared enough to look there.

But the class had changed.

It now moved around two gravitational centers: Dev and Rudra.

Brothers.

And rivals.

Dev, the elder, was effortless in everything—his smile, his posture, his cricket swing, even the way he wore his uniform. He had charisma that made teachers fond and classmates loyal. He didn't try hard, and maybe that's why everyone tried to get closer to him.

Rudra, on the other hand, was sharp. Clean. Exact. He was precise in his notes, focused in class, and ruthless with his timing during tests. His presence wasn't loud—it was commanding. He didn't need admiration; he demanded respect.

But what separated them most was a number.

One.

Rudra was always first.

Dev was always second.

It wasn't said aloud, but it was there—in every result, every ranking board, every half-praised announcement from a teacher.

"Brilliant, Rudra. And Dev... only two marks behind this time. So close!"

So close. Always.

That difference, however small, created a crack no one dared address. Some days, they were brothers in every sense—laughing, walking home together, playfully shoving each other in the corridor.

Other days, their silence was thick enough to divide the classroom in two.

Whispers about their rivalry spread like mist.

"Rudra corrected Dev in front of the teacher."

"Dev took Rudra's cricket team captaincy last year."

"They like the same girl, maybe?"

Aarav watched it all—not from the sidelines, but from a strange, invisible place in between.

He didn't belong to either camp. But that made him useful.

He was neutral territory. Safe passage. The quiet courier.

"What do Rudra talk about me."

"Did dev bothers me. What are his plans."

More than the Dev and Rudra their respective team was more interested in such talks.

Aarav never offered. But he never refused either.

Because he had learned something early on:

Invisibility can be power—if you know how to observe.

He didn't speak much, but he listened deeply. He remembered who said what, who borrowed from whom, who avoided eye contact, who smiled a little longer. Aarav read the room like others read textbooks.

He could sense the tension when Rudra walked in two minutes late and Dev didn't look up.

He noticed the sarcasm in Dev's jokes when Rudra was within earshot.

He saw how Dev's followers laughed louder when Rudra was quiet.

The class didn't just choose sides. They lived them.

But Aarav had something that neither Dev nor Rudra quite understood.

He had a quiet comfort with the girls.

It wasn't strategy. It wasn't charm. It was just... natural.

Aarav had grown up with a girl his age—Pooja, the daughter of his mother's close friend. They had played together before school uniforms meant anything. That familiarity never vanished. It turned into conversation, notes passed without hesitation, shared textbooks, and quiet jokes about assignments.

Through Pooja, other girls slowly included him. Sharanya, who liked his diagram work. Nimmi, who teased him for his handwriting. He became the one they could ask for an extra pencil or summary of a missed lesson.

Most boys didn't understand this. A few admired it.

Many mocked it.

They whispered, smirked, nudged each other when Aarav was seen talking to a girl.

But Aarav had grown past letting whispers define him.

Then came his birthday.

His mother, unaware of school politics, planned a small celebration and invited everyone. But it was the girls who showed up first—eager, excited, real.

They brought handmade cards, colourful sketchbooks, chocolates.

They danced to Bollywood songs in the narrow hall.

They screamed the birthday song so loud the neighbor came to check if something was wrong.

They played musical chairs using plastic stools and made Aarav sit in the middle like a prince.

Some boys came, a little awkward, watching from the edge. A few eventually joined in. But the mood had already been set.

That evening, Aarav wasn't neutral. He wasn't between two poles.

He was centered.

Seen. Celebrated.

And it didn't go unnoticed.

Some boys later joked about the "girl gang party."

Some stopped calling him for cricket.

Others eyed him with subtle resentment.

But Aarav didn't care. Because in a class full of invisible walls, he had built a window.

As sixth standard moved on, Aarav saw it all—the tension between Dev and Rudra, the shifting loyalties of classmates, the rise of quiet jealousy, and the way power didn't always roar.

Sometimes, it whispered.

And he understood something more clearly now:

"Those who stand at the top are always watched.

But the one standing in between—he sees everything."

"Not all wars are loud; some begin with glances."

CHAPTER FOUR

BELL-BOTTOMS AND BOARD EXAMS

Seventh standard came with whispers and weight.

It was the first time Aarav heard the term "board exams" with seriousness. Teachers stopped smiling after November. Notes were thicker. Tests became weekly rituals. And the word revision began haunting students even in their dreams.

But among all the stress, something—or rather, someone—arrived like a breeze through a suffocating room.

Vinay Sir.

The day he entered the class, the corridor fell silent for reasons no one could explain. He wasn't loud. He wasn't angry. He was simply... present.

He walked in with crisp shirts always tucked, pens arranged neatly in his chest pocket, and bell-bottom pants that whispered confidence with every stride. Tall and sharp-featured, he looked less like a teacher and more like someone who belonged in a film scene—chalk in one hand, charisma in the other.

"Good morning. I'm Vinay. I'm not here to help you pass math," he said, pacing slowly.
"I'm here to make sure math doesn't pass you."

A few chuckled nervously. Aarav didn't laugh. He was already watching the man's every movement.

The way he opened his notebook. The angle at which he wrote on the blackboard. The impossibly beautiful handwriting that made even equations look poetic.

Aarav was never weak in math, but he had never felt drawn to it either. Until now.

Not everyone adored him.

Some of the girls whispered that he was too self-absorbed. That he showed off. That he always paid more attention to students who took his tuition classes outside school.

And yes, there were subtle favors. His tuition kids always got called up to solve first. They received nods of approval when others were told to "revise again."

But even those who criticized him couldn't deny his grip on the class.

He made triangles interesting.

He made algebra theatrical.

He made learning feel cool.

And he had a thing for nicknames.

"Whity! Why is your answer looking so pale?"

"Chubby, What did you eate at lunch today."

The class would laugh—and it was laughter that felt warm, not cruel.

Aarav, however, hadn't been nicknamed yet. He was still under the radar.

He had a special way of regarding by giving stars on evaluation. All died to get those and always talked about stars after evaluation. He also mentioned Neat for those who handled books and writing profoundly.

That changed one Wednesday.

Vinay Sir glanced at the first row and pointed.

"You—yes, you, first bench. Aarav, right? Go to the staff room and bring the giant geometry toolbox. It's taller than you. Don't drop it—we have only one set."

The class chuckled. Aarav grinned shyly and stood up.

The geometry box was infamous. Almost the size of a cricket bat case, it contained a monstrous compass, set squares, a rusting protractor the size of a steering wheel, and chalk compartments built like ammo storage.

He carried it with both hands, arms stiff and trembling. The hallway felt longer than usual. A couple of seniors raised eyebrows. A peon clapped sarcastically.

But when he placed it gently on the table in front of Vinay Sir, the man smilcd.

"See? Not all heroes wear capes. Some carry compasses."

The room burst into laughter. Aarav... smiled wider than he had in weeks.

Around the same time, the school inaugurated something that felt like a step into the future—the computer lab.

Five clunky desktops in a small glass-paned room. The monitors buzzed faintly, the keyboards were hard, and the mouse had trackballs underneath. For most students, it was a curiosity. For teachers, a glorified headache.

But for Vinay Sir and Shashank Sir—the computer teacher—it was their private playground.

Every lunch break, after the last bite of tiffin and a short walk to the gate, a delivery boy from Udupi Hotel arrived with packets of dosa and coconut chutney.

Vinay Sir and Shashank Sir would vanish into the lab with their food—and then, the real game began.

Need for Speed.

Aarav saw it once—accidentally. Through the thin glass of the lab door, he noticed the screen flash, the car revving, the digital dust spinning on the screen. Laughter erupted inside the room as one of them lost a race.

From that day on, Aarav timed his hand wash routine during lunch to align with their gaming break.

He would walk past the lab slowly, sometimes standing near the window pretending to adjust his shoelace, just for a peek.
He watched as Vinay Sir controlled the car with ease, one hand finishing a dosa, the other on the keyboard.

Aarav longed to challenge him.

He wasn't a beginner. He had played NFS at his cousin's house in Belgavi. He knew shortcuts. He knew the turbo keys. He knew how to drift corners and beat the countdown.

And somewhere deep inside, he whispered to himself:

"One race. Just one. I can beat him."

But that moment never came.

No invitation. No mention. No chance.

Just a silent fan watching his teacher race pixels between bites of dosa.

And strangely... that was enough.

Because Aarav wasn't learning only equations.

He was learning how passion makes anything cool.

He was learning that confidence can be quiet. That respect doesn't have to be loud. That style isn't in clothes or talk—it's in presence.

Vinay Sir was the first teacher who made Aarav think:

"Maybe I don't have to be the best.
Maybe I just need to be me, done right."
And for a boy who had spent years trying to disappear...
That was everything.

"Sometimes, a teacher doesn't teach subjects—he teaches you how to be."

CHAPTER FIVE

THE NEW TOPPERS

New students rarely made a ripple. They entered mid-year, mumbled their names in front of the class, and quietly faded into the background—struggling to catch up with chapters already finished and friendships already formed.

But that year, three new girls walked into the classroom and changed everything.

Ananya. Sana. Mira.

They stood at the front of the class like three pieces of a different world. One wore her confidence on her sleeve, the other carried poetry in her eyes, and the third... she didn't need to try. She was already first.

From the moment she introduced herself, Ananya didn't need loudness or charm. She had something rarer—clarity. Her voice was soft but firm. She looked teachers in the eye. She answered questions before they finished asking. And by the end of the first weekly test, she was rank one.

It wasn't just a win—it was a shift in gravity.

For a class long ruled by the silent war between Dev and Rudra, this was disruption. And it wasn't just academic.

Rudra noticed first.

No one said it. But everyone saw it.

He began arriving to class a few minutes earlier than usual. He stopped asking unnecessary questions. His sarcasm in class debates softened.

And every now and then, his eyes would linger—not just at the blackboard, but at the girl scribbling notes beside him.

Aarav saw it too.

The small exchanges. The accidental glances. The moment when Ananya dropped her eraser and Rudra bent to pick it up before she could.

It wasn't romance.

Not yet.

It was attention. And for someone like Rudra, attention was never casual.

Sana, on the other hand, came like a firecracker. Bold, unapologetic, and loud in a way the class wasn't used to from girls. She cracked jokes. Interrupted the boys. Teased Dev without fear. Her energy filled every corner of the room.

Mira was different. Dreamy-eyed, always doodling in the corners of her notebooks, she spent more time looking out the window than in it. But when she spoke, her words had weight—quiet but clever, like they were filtered through thought.

Together, the three created a new kind of presence—not competitive, not threatening, but simply impossible to ignore.

And the boys noticed. Oh, they noticed.

The backbenchers whispered. The front-benchers adjusted their hairstyles. Trump cards stopped flying during breaks. Even the chalk fights became a little more restrained.

Aarav didn't speak to them much.

But he watched.

Ananya's neat notes. Sana's loud laughter echoing through the corridors. Mira tracing patterns on the desk with her fingers while pretending to listen.

He liked observing from a distance—not out of shyness, but because he understood people better that way. And somewhere in the shifting tides, he sensed a coming storm.

Because in a class already divided by invisible walls, three new voices meant three new reactions.

And one of those voices—Ananya's—was beginning to find a rhythm that matched Rudra's silence.

The rest of the class?

They were starting to notice, too.

"A name unspoken can still carry the weight of blame."

CHAPTER SIX

The Lesson, the Laughter, and the Slap

Some lessons leave a mark not in your notebook—but across your face, in your memory, and on your self-worth.

It was a slow afternoon.

The kind where the ceiling fans groaned louder than the students. Where the chalk dust seemed to hang in the sunlight like a haze of boredom. The post-lunch lull made everything feel far away—dream-like, muted.

Aarav was seated in his usual first-row spot, his arms folded across his notebook. He wasn't sleepy. He just wasn't present.

The teacher for the next period entered the class with her usual grace. Ms. Rajeshwari. An elegant woman with expressive eyes and an almost poetic voice. She wasn't the kind of teacher who shouted. Her strength came from silence, from the weight her words carried.

"We're reading a lesson today about Mother Teresa," she said softly.

The class sat up just a little.

She began reading aloud from the textbook. Her voice carried calm and gravity.

"She found the dying beggar lying on the side of the street, soaked in filth.

She took him in her arms. Cleaned his wounds.

She washed him with her own hands. She bathed him..."

And then—

A snicker.

One. Then two. Then a low ripple of chuckles.

Aarav turned.

He knew that laugh. It came from the corner near the windows—the usual suspects, boys who treated everything sacred like a joke. Their shoulders trembled. One covered his mouth. Another leaned back, whispering into someone else's ear.

And then the one with the cracked voice said it:

"Washing? What kind of love is that, huh? Romantic Teresa!"

The class erupted—not in laughter, but in awkwardness. A few smiled. Most went pale. Aarav didn't laugh. He sat still, his stomach turning.

Ms. Rajeshwari froze.

She didn't speak. She closed the textbook slowly. Her hands trembled—just a little—but her eyes didn't blink.

She stepped back from the podium, her voice barely above a whisper:

"I came here to teach you compassion.
Not to have you mock it.
I will not teach this lesson to boys who laugh at pain."

And she left the room.

No slamming. No yelling. Just silence. The kind that made you want to hide inside your desk.

No one spoke.

Then came the sound everyone feared—

The footsteps.

Firm. Heavy. Unmistakable.

Principal Dinesh.

A former army major, he walked in like a command. Ray-Ban aviators still on, shirt tucked with ironed lines so sharp they could slice paper, and his infamous oiled bamboo stick held like a baton of justice.

Fifteen minutes later, the temperature dropped in the room—not because of weather, but because of the man who walked in.

Principal Dinesh.

Retired Major. Aviator sunglasses still on. Shirt tucked tighter than any exam answer sheet. His oiled bamboo stick tapped once on the floor before he spoke.

"Your teacher left the class mid-lesson. She left crying."

No one breathed.

"You think this is a joke? You think social work, human dignity... is funny?"

He scanned the room like a soldier in a trench.

Then he said:

"Tell me who laughed... or the entire class will be reported. Including your grades."

Still, no hands.

No courage.

Not even from the boys who had laughed.

And then, he pointed at Aarav.

"You—front row. You must've heard everything."

Aarav stood, startled.

"Sir... I heard laughter. But I didn't see who—"

"Enough!"

The slap came fast. Loud. Open-palmed.

The room exploded into silence.

Aarav didn't cry.

But the sting was more than just on his cheek. It was the sting of injustice. Of being made the sacrificial example because he happened to sit near the fire, not inside it.

Dinesh stormed out. Ms. Rajeshwari followed quietly, her eyes refusing to meet the students'.

And just like that... the class was left stunned.

No one laughed now.

An hour later, Aarav was called to the staff room.

He hesitated before walking in. Teachers were murmuring among themselves, glancing his way.

Ms. Rajeshwari sat at a desk with the same textbook—now closed, the red silk ribbon still marking the page.

She looked up at him with sadness, not anger.

"Aarav," she said gently, "you sit right in front of them. Please tell me who it was. Just the names."

He stared at the floor.

His palms were sweating. His throat dry.

He knew who had laughed.

He knew exactly where the whisper had begun.

But he also knew this:

He couldn't turn on his bench mates. Not because they didn't deserve it. But because he didn't want to become like them—throwing someone under the bus just to save himself.

"Ma'am," he said softly, "I was in the front row.
The laughter came from the back.
I... I honestly couldn't see who started it."

She sighed. Leaned back.

She knew he was lying. Or at least withholding.

But she didn't press further.

Instead, she nodded.

"You may go."

He walked out slowly.

He didn't feel proud.

He didn't feel noble.

He just felt... tired.

The day didn't end with the slap.

It only started there.

By the time the final bell rang, Aarav thought it was over. That maybe his silence in the staff room had closed the chapter.

But it hadn't.

It had only moved the scene to a different stage.

A peon entered the classroom, looked directly at Aarav, then turned to the backbenchers.

"Dinesh sir wants these boys. Now."

He read out the names—eight in total, all boys. Aarav's name was the first.

Some of the others smirked nervously. A few tried to whisper "we're all in this together" lines. But Aarav's jaw was tight.

He wasn't even angry anymore.

Just... numb.

The corridor to the Principal's office felt longer that day. The air was heavier. The walls seemed to listen.

When they entered, Major Dinesh was standing beside his massive teak desk. His aviators rested on the table. His sleeves were rolled up. And the oiled bamboo stick glistened under the fan.

His eyes didn't hold rage. They held purpose. Discipline. Old-school justice.

"Since none of you had the courage to confess," he said, "all of you will share the consequences."

No pleas.

No questions.

Just silence.

And then... the first strike.

Crack!

The stick came down across the back of the tallest boy. He yelped and jumped forward. The others gasped.

Then the next.

Then another.

One by one, the boys received clean, punishing strikes. Some tried to dodge. Some attempted to run around the table.

It didn't matter.

Dinesh Sir was fast. Efficient. Merciless.

Boys rolled across the granite floor, their shirts half-out, knees scuffed, trying to avoid the next hit.

It looked like a scene from an old army drill, only without protection. No one was spared.

Not even Aarav.

When the stick came for him, he stood still for the first hit. It landed across his back, a fiery sting.

The second, he tried to step back—but slipped. Landed on his elbows.

The third hit his leg as he tried to crawl to the side.

No words.

No cries.

Only the dull rhythm of punishment and the whimper of boys too shocked to react.

After it was done, Dinesh sir spoke once more:

"You'll forget this pain. But I hope you remember what led to it."

And then, as simply as he had begun, he dismissed them with a wave.

"Go. Back to class."

Aarav walked out limping slightly, shirt damp with sweat, palm marks visible through thin fabric.

The others were silent.

There were no jokes now.

No teasing.

Not even eye contact.

They were just boys stripped of their pride, walking side by side in shame and ache—some guilty, some not, all punished the same.

That evening, Aarav didn't talk much.

He convinced his sisters not the talk about this to his mother.

He didn't tell his mother.

He didn't even look in the mirror.

He just lay on his bed, his cheek still faintly marked from the slap, his back sore, his heart... heavier.

He thought about how easy it was to get caught in something you didn't start.

How fast a moment could collapse into memory.

And how being silent could still lead you to the center of the storm.

"When someone rises, the silence below starts to rumble."

CHAPTER SEVEN

THE GAMBIT

Sometimes, the most dangerous things don't happen in the open—they happen quietly, behind half-closed rickshaw flaps, between casual words spoken with too much comfort.

That's how the whispers began.

At first, it was subtle— "Did you see the driver smile too much again today?"

Then the stories grew darker. Someone in the neighbouring village overheard what the rickshaw driver said to another girl. Someone noticed he took longer to reach the next stop, though Ananya had already gotten down at school.

And then came the line that crossed everything:

"He tried to flirt when he talked to her about her schedule."

That's when it changed.

Ananya also because of her routine with driver, she was easy going smiled at him while getting down. And that smile was seen by a younger student.

But for Rudra—who heard it from someone two years younger, a quiet boy who shared the same rickshaw route and had noticed the incident on the way to his own stop. He also described how the driver had started impressing her by planning romantic songs during the ride. And even Ananya had started humming the songs and enjoying the ride.

Rudra didn't react in front of others.

He just stood up from his bench.

And walked out during break.

What happened next was only pieced together by fragments of stories, shared in corners of the school with hushed awe.

The driver, as always, continued his daily route after dropping Ananya.

It was midday. The sun was sharp. The road was nearly empty—just a stretch of dry dust, bordered by tamarind trees and the occasional bleating of a goat.

He pulled over under a neem tree to fix the loose tarp on the side of the rickshaw.

And that's when Rudra and three boys appeared.

No shouting.

No introduction.

Just movement.

"You think nobody's watching?" Rudra said, voice low. "You think we won't find out?"

The driver blinked, confused, stammered something about "just helping" and "nothing happened."

But Rudra didn't wait for explanations.

He stepped forward, grabbed the man by the collar, and shoved him against the side of the rickshaw. The driver's head hit the metal frame with a dull thud.

The others surrounded him.

No fists yet. Just presence.

Terrifying presence.

Rudra's eyes were sharper than ever.

"Next time if you look at her that way.. "
"You won't be driving. You'll be crawling."

"If you ever lay your eyes on her like that again... I promise, driving will be the last thing you'll worry about. You'll be lucky if you can crawl."

The driver nodded furiously, terrified.

Rudra leaned in close and whispered something no one else heard.

And just like that—it was over.

The boys walked away.

The driver never returned to that route again.

Another rickshaw came the next day. A younger one. Quiet. No smiles.

Ananya didn't ask questions.

But she knew.

She walked to class with the same silence as always. But her eyes lingered on Rudra for a half-second longer than usual.

He didn't look at her.

He just adjusted his bag strap and turned the page of his textbook.

Aarav heard the whole story in parts.

First from someone in Rudra's group.

Then from a junior who saw the bruised driver at the tea shop, muttering about "mad school boys."

He didn't know whether to be afraid of Rudra or admire him.

But one thing was clear—this wasn't just a school rivalry anymore.

This was something else.

Something that made people stand up, even when it wasn't their fight.

Ananya never thanked Rudra.

She didn't need to.

Because from that day, something shifted.

She began sharing her pencil when he forgot his.

She saved a seat for him during assembly without being asked.

And once, during group work, she passed him a notebook already labelled with both their names.

It wasn't romance.

Not yet.

But it was respect, and maybe even something more.

"Not all battles are public; some are fought for the ones who never knew."

CHAPTER EIGHT

THE CYCLE BELL

Not all feelings arrive with declarations.

Some arrive slowly—like a tune stuck in your head. Like a glance that lingers a second longer than it should. Like a bell that rings, not once, but just enough to say, "I see you."

That's how it began with Sana.

She wasn't like Ananya, whose silence was intelligent and heavy, or Mira, who floated like a thought in the breeze. Sana was wind herself—quick, bold, and delightfully unfiltered. She teased boys without fear, gave side glances to teachers when they tried too hard, and walked like the corridor was her stage.

And Aarav?

He barely spoke to her.

But he noticed everything.

How she always carried a red pen even though no teacher ever asked for one.

How she folded the edge of every notebook page like a tiny triangle.

How she sang old songs under her breath while waiting for class to begin.

It was nothing dramatic.

But slowly, she became a rhythm in Aarav's day.

And Aarav, quiet, observant, and emotionally tucked away in his own world, began trying small, subtle ways to be seen—not by everyone, just by her.

It started with the cycle bell.

His school route took him past the cluster of homes where Sana lived. Their timings weren't always in sync, but sometimes—just sometimes—he'd spot her walking with her bag slung and a tiffin bag on one hand, laughing with Nimmi or Mira.

One day, he was behind her lane, and without thinking, he rang his cycle bell—not once, not twice, but in a peculiar, playful rhythm.

Ting-ting. Ting. Ting-ting.

He didn't stop or slow down. He just passed by, heart racing like the cycle wheels under him.

He wasn't sure why he did it.

But the next time he saw her in school, she looked at him curiously. Not mockingly. Not smiling. Just... curious.

"Was that your cycle near the bakery yesterday?" she asked suddenly in class.

Aarav blinked.

He nodded. Slowly.

Sana squinted at him.

"You have a weird bell style," she said.

And then, as if that was the most normal conversation in the world, she turned back to her desk and started humming again.

Aarav couldn't stop smiling.

From then on, the cycle bell became his language.

Whenever he passed her lane, he'd ring it in the same odd rhythm. Sometimes once. Sometimes twice. He never waited to see if she noticed. That wasn't the point.

It was enough to feel like he existed in her world, even if it was just for three seconds a day.

He didn't know if it was love.

But it was something sweet. Something only his heart understood.

And in a life full of chaos, politics, punishments, and invisible wars, this one feeling was soft. Gentle. Just his.

Aarav had always floated between groups, between glances, between words unsaid.

But there was one person at school who never made him feel halfway.

Mrs. Meenakshi, the Hindi teacher.

She wasn't loud. Didn't walk in with perfume trailing behind her like some others. But she had the kind of silence that felt safe. And in her class, Aarav always felt like he belonged.

One day, she asked a simple question about muhavarein—Hindi idioms.

The class was half-asleep, the air still, and the chalk on the board barely visible through sunlight.

Aarav raised his hand.

Slowly. Reluctantly.

And when she called on him, he answered—not to impress, but because he understood.

She smiled—a full smile, not the half ones teachers usually gave.

"Bahut accha kaha, Aarav."

Very well said, Aarav.

For the rest of the class, she asked him more questions.

He responded. Confident. Clear.

And for a fleeting moment, the entire class watched him, not as a filler in the first row, but as someone who stood out.

But the whispers came soon after.

"Favourite student, huh?"

"He must be carrying her notebooks after class."

Some laughed quietly.

Others just looked at him like he had broken a rule he wasn't even told existed.

That day, Aarav learned something—

Even admiration could make you a target.

Later, when she called him out gently after class, she said just one thing:

"Let them talk. You keep learning."

She never protected him loudly.

But in her silence, Aarav always felt safe.

And in a school full of shifting loyalties, that made her his favourite.

"To be seen without asking, is the rarest kind of support."

CHAPTER NINE

THE ROOM WITH THE RAY-BAN

The door to the principal's office had always felt heavier than it should. Not just in weight—but in what it held behind it.

Aarav hesitated. His name had been called during the last period. No note, no warning—just a soft, stern "Principal's office" from the peon at the door. The walk through the corridor had felt longer than usual.

He knocked.

"Come in," said the familiar deep voice.

Principal Dinesh was seated at his usual spot—back straight, shirt crisp, his signature Ray-Ban aviators resting beside a thick file. The oiled bamboo stick still hung on the wall behind him like a relic from another era. But today, there was something different in the air. No fire. No fury. Just stillness.

Aarav entered, his eyes downcast.

"You burgers are grown up now," Dinesh said, not looking up from his file. "These chaps are good at studies. You—" he paused and raised his eyes, "—you have far to go."

Aarav felt his chest tighten. He tried to speak, to justify.

"Sir, I didn't mean to—" he started, his voice barely above a whisper, shaky, stammering under pressure.

But Dinesh didn't let him finish.

"Stop chipping like sparrows and pull up your socks," he said, sharp and sudden, his gaze piercing.

Aarav froze.

There was no anger in Dinesh's tone. But there was weight. Authority. The kind that didn't need to shout to be heard.

"Look," Dinesh continued, softer now, tapping his fingers against the table, "you've been hanging between both ends—trying to be fair, trying to fit in. That never works for long. You can't balance on a sword."

He leaned back, arms folded, the smell of his cigarette from earlier still lingering in the air.

"You don't have to be the best," he said. "But you better be your best. Else, this school will forget you the moment you step out. And trust me, the world outside won't even blink."

Aarav remained silent, absorbing every word. For the first time, the room didn't feel like a place of punishment. It felt like a mirror.

"Don't wait for people to choose your side," Dinesh said, pointing gently with two fingers. "Decide who you are, and stay there. Whether they like it or not."

Then, almost casually, he reached for his aviators and stood up.

"You can go now."

Aarav didn't know what to say. So he simply nodded and turned.

The door clicked shut behind him, but the words stayed. Clearer than any scolding. Sharper than any slap.

"Stop chipping like sparrows and pull up your socks."

It wasn't a warning. It was a wake-up call.

And Aarav heard it loud and clear.

"Some lessons don't echo in corridors—they settle in your spine."

CHAPTER TEN

BETWEEN SONGS AND SUNDAYS

School wasn't always about marks and rivalries.

Some days, it was about how long you could stretch a break without getting caught. Or how creatively you could express a crush without actually saying anything. Or whether you could listen to the last two overs of an India-Pakistan match without the teacher noticing.

Aarav loved those days the most.

The classroom had its own politics, but in between those tense silences and invisible lines, a strange language of mischief evolved. The boys had a system. An entire unspoken code of behavior.

When a teacher was five minutes late, someone would volunteer as the "door guard". Always the boldest of the group. He'd stand outside casually—hand on the handle, eyes scanning both ends of the corridor.

Inside, it was chaos.

Trump cards would be pulled from pencil boxes—Shaktimaan, Undertaker, Sachin Tendulkar. Fights would break out over whether "Glow Power" beats "Smash Power". Aarav never played. But he loved watching—especially the way serious expressions melted into childlike grins the moment the game began.

Once, someone even smuggled a small radio into school during a crucial cricket match. It was hidden inside a lunchbox. They listened with the earphones split across two heads while pretending to read from a science textbook.

"Sachin hit a six!"

"Shut up, madam's coming!"

"No, it's just Hindi sir."

Aarav always loved to be with them some way or other. But he sat next to them—close enough to hear the whispers. And that was enough.

But Sundays—Sundays were serious.

Every few weeks, the school would schedule friendly cricket matches with nearby schools. No trophies. No announcements. Just pure supremacy battles.

It wasn't about who won—it was about which group of boys were better. Dev's team. Rudra's team. Sometimes, combined. Sometimes, opposed. The winning amount went to Udupi hotel for the delightful breakfast for all the team members.

The matches were sweaty. Loud. Full of arguments and poor umpiring.

Aarav?

He didn't play.

He was almost always the umpire.

No one asked. He volunteered. Not because he couldn't bat or bowl—but because he liked watching from the center without being in the spotlight.

He could observe reactions, body language, cheating attempts, hidden smiles.

And in football periods, the same story.

"Aarav, you'll be goalkeeper, okay?"

"Sure," he'd nod.

Not because he loved stopping goals.

But because it was the only position where he could stay still and still be a part of everything.

Then came the monsoon months.

The river near the school would overflow, water turning murky and wild. On certain stormy days, the principal would walk into assembly, and the school would hold its breath.

"Due to rising water levels and potential flood alerts..."

That was all it took.

Cheering. Clapping. Bags zipped in record time. Plans to meet at someone's house, to play, to watch a movie, or just do nothing.

For Aarav, those holidays were magic.

Unexpected, sweet, and deserved.

After school, another kind of chaos unfolded.

Tuition sprints.

As soon as the bell rang, kids became athletes. Bags were flung over shoulders, slippers slapped the floor, and cycles zipped through the main road. Aarav never understood the rush.

He attended only one tuition, reluctantly. But he loved watching the race more than joining it. The way classmates transformed from bored students to sprinting legends in five seconds was fascinating.

And in between it all were the songs.

Not the ones in the textbook.

But the ones sung just loud enough to reach the right ears.

"Raat ko Aaunga mein tujhe le jaaunga mein"

"Hatta Saawan ki Ghatta"

"Yeh kya bolti tu.."

"Humdum soniyo re.."

And the favourite one "Kitna Pyaara tujhe rab ne baanaya"

Usually boys, sometimes girls. Always sung casually. Always aimed carefully.

Aarav never sang.

But he smiled when he heard it.

Because even unspoken things had a place in their world.

And in a school full of punishments, rivalries, and academic pressure, these stolen moments of song, sun, and silence were where they all came alive.

"Sometimes, a rhythm says more than words ever could."

CHAPTER ELEVEN

THE TAMARIND RAIN

It began, like most beautiful disasters in school do, with a tree.

A large, rough-barked tamarind tree stood near the side wall of the school grounds—part forgotten by the staff, fully claimed by the students. It wasn't just a tree. It was a secret. A ritual. A mid-break mission.

One day, during the short break after second period, someone threw a slipper at its branches. Not out of hunger—just out of instinct.

Thud.

Down came a shower of tamarinds—twisting, bouncing, and rolling across the cement floor like marbles freed from a bag.

A few boys ran to gather them. As usual, expectations were low. Tamarinds were supposed to be sour, mouth-twitching, nose-wrinkling sour. But not this time.

"It's sweet!" one of the boys shouted, eyes wide, chewing with wonder.

"Really sweet, da!"

"Ninoun esta sala heleni, da anbyad anta!" (Other shouting Not to use "da...")

The word spread faster than the bell.

The tamarind was magical—ripe, warm from the sun, and naturally sweetened by the late-monsoon humidity.

And when some were passed to the girls, everything changed.

Mira crinkled her nose and smiled.

Sana bit one, made a dramatic face, then reached for another.

And then Ananya, curious but cautious, accepted a few from the edge of a bench.

"Do you have more?" she asked softly, lips pursed from the tang.

A few boys exchanged looks.

Challenge accepted.

Lunch break.

Aarav was mid-bite into his chapati when it began.

Plop.

A tamarind pod hit the floor near Mira's feet.

She squealed.

Then—another.

Then two more.

And within seconds, the class turned into a battlefield.

Boys ducked behind benches, girls screamed and ran. Some tamarind pods still had their shells on. Some were squished, leaving sticky trails on the floor, the desks, even the blackboard.

Someone climbed the window grill. Someone else slid under the teacher's desk like it was war. Even Aarav, who normally avoided the center of chaos, got hit on the arm—direct shot by Sana, who just smirked and ran.

Ananya didn't throw any.

But she laughed—really laughed.

Head tilted back, hands on her stomach, face flushed red.

And that... made it worth it.

Then came the turning point.

The bell rang.

And so did trouble.

Because the next teacher on the timetable was Mr. Gopal, a man whose patience was thinner than a geometry sheet. He walked in mid-storm—and froze.

His polished leather shoes crushed a tamarind shell as he stepped forward.

The room went dead silent.

Tamarind pods everywhere. On desks. On the floor. On the teacher's chair. On the window sill. One stuck to the back of the class noticeboard like a forgotten bullet.

"Out," he said.

"Everyone. OUT."

No protests. No explanations.

Forty students walked out in silence and formed a line across the corridor wall—uniforms stained, fingers sticky, faces somewhere between pride and regret.

Even Ananya was there.

Even Dev and Rudra.

Even Aarav—who stood beside Sana, unsure whether to smile or scold her for that well-aimed shot.

They stood in the corridor like soldiers after a failed coup. Some were giggling. Some were nervous. One boy tried to blame it on a crow.

But deep inside, every one of them knew...

It was worth it.

"Not every act needs an audience to be remembered."

CHAPTER TWELVE

REHEARSALS AND REJECTIONS

The announcement came during assembly.

"This year's valedictory function will feature performances from outgoing and junior students. Selected teams will perform during the final ceremony."

Nothing too unusual—until one detail turned the air electric.

"The girls from Class 9, led by Ananya, will present a Bollywood mashup choreographed by Prabhavati herself."

That's all it took.

By lunch break, the classroom was buzzing.

"Bole Chudiyan and Dola Re mix, bro!"

"Prabhavati Teacher teaching them steps? It's serious, then."

"We can't just sit and clap, da. We need a boys' performance too!"

And just like that, a rebellion was born.

The motive wasn't artistic.

It wasn't even about stage time.

It was, as most boy-led initiatives go, about escaping classes under the noble guise of rehearsals.

Dev wasn't interested. Rudra stayed aloof. But the rest? They were in.

"Let's do a dance group. Aarav will be the captain."

Aarav froze mid-sip of water.

"Me? I don't even dance."

"Exactly. That's why you won't overdo it," someone laughed.

And before he could protest, his fate was sealed—with backslaps and paper scraps that said "Boys Dance Team - Finalised."

The next 15 days became chaos.

Six boys. One borrowed tape recorder. Eight A-size batteries.

Each brought from home in secret, stuffed into bags between textbooks and tiffin boxes.

The classroom became their rehearsal hall.

Chairs pushed aside, school belts tied around heads like sweatbands, and some of the worst dance moves to ever disgrace a tiled floor.

One boy only knew Govinda-style hip thrusts.

Another couldn't remember the steps after 10 seconds.

Aarav? He stood in the back, trying to copy moves and failing gloriously.

And yet... they had fun.

So much fun.

They danced on:

Breaks

Late PT periods

Empty pre-lunch slots when a teacher didn't show up

They argued about songs. Voted on jeans vs. uniform pants. Laughed until their stomachs hurt.

For the first time, the class felt like one team.

No Dev. No Rudra. No toppers. No backbenchers.

Just sweaty, awkward boys laughing at their own missteps.

Then came the selection day.

They performed their piece in front of the cultural committee.

It lasted two minutes and twenty-nine seconds.

No one clapped.

Later that week, the list was put up.

The boys' dance team was not selected.

Some felt bad because they took it serious unknowingly and criticized Aarav for not making it. Some knew what was it all about and enjoyed.

Because by then, they had shared more than rehearsals.

They had shared water bottles, stickers, music, backward glances, and the kind of carefree brotherhood that only lives in dusty classrooms and teenage laughs.

Aarav, who had never led anything before, wasn't upset.

He felt something stronger than pride.

He felt included.

"*Sometimes the page speaks what the heart never dared.*"

39

CHAPTER THIRTEEN

THE FINAL BELL

Summer arrived not with heat—but with tension.

Board exams were on the list, but ninth standard results loomed like a storm cloud. Those who once spent their days chasing chalk fights and tamarind treats now sat with books twice their size and pens that ran out of ink too soon.

The famous bandhu guide was the tool for each problem. Student even renamed a sir name as bandhu for his reference to it for each answer.

The school, once noisy with mischief, now echoed with a different sound:

The scratch of nibs on paper.

The countdown of timed dictations.

The anxiety of speed-writing books filled to improve exam pace.

And the quiet dread of whether it would all be enough.

Aarav sat through long summer classes, sweat dripping down his back as he filled page after page in speed-writing notebooks. His fingers cramped. His eyes burned. But he never stopped.

There were no more group rehearsals. No back-bench trumpet-card duels. Even the cycle bell had lost its usual rhythm.

Everyone was serious now.

Focused.

Distant.

Each dictation lasted nearly an hour.

The teachers, once warm and lenient, had turned into military commanders. Every punctuation mark mattered. Every missed word was a warning. Even Vinay Sir had dropped his charming nicknames.

"You won't get extra time in the board exam. Either keep up, or stay behind."

There were no complaints. No backtalk. Only the sound of 40 pens racing a ticking clock.

Aarav and his friend Basu joined for combined study, Basu was better than Aarav. He was good at studies.

The countdown had begun—not to a performance, but to a parting.

In those final weeks, Aarav found himself growing quieter. Not because he had nothing to say—but because he had too much he didn't know how to express.

One thought lingered constantly, like a melody only he could hear:

"What does Sana feel?"

He had never told her what he felt. Not directly.

There were smiles. Glances. That one conversation about his cycle bell. A shared laugh during the tamarind incident. A few awkward moments when their hands brushed while passing papers.

But words?

None.

And now, time was slipping away.

On the final day, after the last bell rang, Aarav walked back to his desk with a plan.

From his bag, he pulled out a scrapbook—the kind students filled with memories, farewell messages, silly doodles, and quotes that felt too big for their age.

One by one, he passed it around.

"Write something," he said to each friend. "Anything. A line. A drawing. A memory."

There were jokes. Bad sketches. Messages that began with "Don't forget me" and ended with "We'll meet in college."

And then, at the end of it all, he walked toward Sana.

She was tying her shoelace, half-smiling, half-exhausted from the long summer.

Aarav held out the scrapbook, his hand trembling slightly.

"You're the last one to fill this," he said.

She raised an eyebrow.
Took the book slowly.

Aarav looked at her—really looked at her—one final time. The red pen she always carried tucked behind her ear. That little triangle fold at the corner of her notebook. Her eyes... steady.

And then he whispered, barely loud enough:

"Write whatever you feel.

For the reason you already know."

He paused, then smiled.

With a dialogue which was of that time.

"Kal ho naa ho..."

Sana blinked. But didn't speak.

She took the book. Pressed it against her chest. And nodded.

Aarav walked away.

He didn't look back.

The bell rang again.

Not to begin a class.

But to end a chapter.

And with it, a boy named Aarav left behind not just a school... but a version of himself that had grown, fallen, fought, smiled, and quietly learned what it meant to live in between.

"He wasn't the loud one. But he was heard."

CHAPTER FOURTEEN

THE CURTAIN

The day of the valedictory function arrived not with a bang, but with a kind of strange, gentle finality. As if even the school itself knew that this was the last act.

The stage was set. Lights tested. White chairs arranged in perfect symmetry across the dusty assembly ground. Juniors ran around with placards. Teachers carried clipboards. The principal's sunglasses, as always, reflected the crowd like a mirror of authority.

Aarav sat on the second row—just close enough to see the stage, just far enough to disappear in the crowd.

He wasn't nervous.

He was just... full.

Full of memories.

Of trump cards and tamarinds.

Of Dev and Rudra.

Of Sana's smirk and Vinay Sir's chalk lines.

Of punishments he didn't deserve, and smiles he never expected.

Of everything in between.

He scanned the girls whispering and fixing each other's hair, juniors rushing to take a seat at their favorite spot.

The mic cracked.

The speakers buzzed.

And the voice of the vice principal echoed:

"We now begin with the final segment... the Awards."

The list was predictable.

Best Sportsman. Best All-Rounder. Most Regular.

Names that everyone knew. Applause that came easily.

And then—

"Best Boy of the Year..."

The mic squealed.

Aarav looked down.

"...is awarded to... Aarav."

The silence was almost surreal.

No applause. No cheers. Just a collective pause.

Then, reluctantly, a few claps. Mostly from teachers. And juniors made the path way.

The class didn't clap.

In fact, they barely looked at him.

And that hurt.

But Aarav stood anyway.

He slowly during the walk looked at Meenakshi Madam, Rajeshwari Madam vinay Sir and all other fraternity, she had smile on their face. He acknowledge them by lowering the head, with his right hand on chest.

He walked to the stage—straight, measured steps. His heart didn't race. His hands didn't shake.

He accepted the certificate. The medal. Touched the feet of all teachers and dignities.

He smiled—not wide, but steady.

And when he turned to face the crowd, he didn't look for his friends. Or his group. Or even Sana.

He looked at the school.

At the building that had held his childhood. At the classrooms that had bruised and built him. At the ground where he had umpired, being bullied from day one, written boards on each function, guarded the goalpost, and once, been hit by tamarind.

He thanked all his teachers mentors and friends.

And he whispered—not aloud, but to himself.

"Thank you."

After the ceremony, as the crowd dispersed and chairs fell out of their neat rows, Aarav stood near the school gate for a moment longer.

Sana passed by—silent, unreadable.

She didn't say anything.

But she handed him the scrapbook.

He didn't open it.
Not yet.
He simply smiled and nodded.
"Take care," she said.
"You too."
And just like that...
The curtain fell.
Not with a roar.
Not with applause.
But with the softest goodbye.

Aarav walked home slowly, with the scrapbook under one arm and the sun behind his back.

His school was now a memory.
His silence, his strength.
And his journey—not perfect, but his own—had only just begun.

The Curtain

Epilogue: The Message

That night, after the farewell function, Aarav didn't go out.

No celebration dinner. No selfies with friends. No schoolbag burning on the terrace like some boys had planned.

He sat in his room, the window open to a warm breeze, the sound of crickets humming over the faint echoes of distant music.

The scrapbook lay in front of him.

Quiet. Closed. Final.

His fingers hovered over the cover.

Inside were messages that made him smile, chuckle, even wince a little.

But it was the last page he hadn't touched yet.

The one Sana had written.

He stared at it.

Part of him wanted to know.

Part of him didn't.

Because what if it said nothing?

What if it was just a thank-you, or a goodbye?

What if it was more than that?

He thought about her laughter.

About the way she said, "Weird bell style."

About the way she threw that tamarind—no warning, no apology.

And the way she looked at him when he handed her the book.

A look that felt like a word she hadn't said.

He exhaled.

Gently opened the last page.

And there it was.

Sana's handwriting—slightly slanted, with ink that looked like she had pressed the pen just a little harder than usual.

"Some things are better unspoken.

But if you really want to know...

I noticed everything too."

–Sana

That was it.

No hearts.
No declarations.
No confusion.
Just clarity.
Aarav closed the book.
He didn't smile immediately.
He just sat there, the night wrapping around him like a pause.
And slowly—slowly—he felt it settle in his chest.
Not joy.
Not sadness.
Just... peace.
Because sometimes, that's all a goodbye needs.
Not fireworks.
Not promises.
Just a single sentence that says:
"You mattered."

"He wasn't the loud one. But he was heard."

Thank You..

Thank you for walking with Aarav through the corridors of childhood,
confusion, and courage.
But Aarav's journey doesn't end here.

What lies beyond the applause,
behind the silence of recognition,
and ahead of his teenage years—
will unfold in the next book...